The school bus comes
At a quarter to eight!

There's a crowd in the road!
And it sure feels good
To wait all together
In our neighborhood.

Why are we waiting?
So we won't be late....

There's a crowd in the road!
Where there wasn't before,
Side by side
At seven forty-four.
The cow and the goat
And the sheep and the horse
And the goose and the pig,
And me, of course!

So the cow looks at me
And the cow says, "Moo!"
And the next thing I know
I'm standing there too!

There's a pig in the road!
And it's easy to see
That the road is the place
For a kid like me.

He's a large pink pig
With a big broad smile
And I'm going out to meet him
In a very short while.

There's a pig in the road!
At the end of the line
As I gobble my toast
At seven thirty-nine.

Then the cow looks at me
And the cow says, "Moo!"
And the next thing I know
There's a pig there too!

There's a goose in the road!
In a gray-feathered gown
Telling barnyard stories
From all over town.

She's walking around
And honking a lot,
She's looking for something
But she won't say what.

There's a goose in the road!
She's down by the tree
As I grab my homework
At seven thirty-three.

Then the cow looks at me
And the cow says, "Moo!"
And the next thing I know
There's a goose there too!

There's a horse in the road!
All ready to go.
He doesn't look sleepy
And he doesn't look slow.

He's twitching his tail
And tossing his mane
He's a handsome horse
(But a little bit vain)—

There's a horse in the road!
And he's full of tricks
As I comb my hair
At seven twenty-six.

But the cow looks at me
And the cow says, "Moo!"
And the next thing I know
There's a horse there too!

There's a sheep in the road!
Where the drive meets the grass,
And there's just enough room
For the cars to pass.

Don't ask me the reason—
I don't have a clue.
She's just standing there
With the other two.

There's a sheep in the road!
With her fleece all clean
As I wash my face
At seven-fifteen.

Then the cow looks at me
And the cow says, "Moo!"
And the next thing I know
There's a sheep there too!

There's a goat in the road!
As plain as can be,
And our paperboy's hiding
Behind a tree.

He's got four white feet
And a fine white beard
He's a gorgeous goat
But it still seems weird—

There's a goat in the road!
At the edge of our drive
As I pull on my socks
At seven-oh-five.

And the next thing I know
There's a goat there too!

Then the cow looks at me
And the cow says, "Moo!"

There's a cow in the road!
She's a big one too,
Browsing on blossoms
Drenched with dew.

To hear the horns
And the screech of brakes
And go to the window
And see— Gosh sakes!

There's a cow in the road!
And it sure is a shock
When I first wake up
At seven o'clock

For Cutter and Gump, with love
R. L.

For Christopher, Matthew, and Jonathan—
this book is for moo.
T. C. P.

This book is a presentation of Newfield Publications, Inc.
Newfield Publications offers book clubs for children from
preschool through high school. For further information write to:
Newfield Publications, Inc., 4343 Equity Drive,
Columbus, Ohio 43228.

Published by arrangement with Dial Books for Young Readers, a division of Penguin Books USA Inc. Newfield Publications is a federally
registered trademark of Newfield Publications, Inc. Weekly Reader is a
federally registered trademark of Weekly Reader Corporation.

Printed in the United States of America.

Published by Dial Books for Young Readers
A Division of Penguin Books USA Inc.
375 Hudson Street
New York, NY 10014

Design by Jane Byers Bierhorst
First Edition
1 3 5 7 9 10 8 6 4 2

Library of Congress Cataloging in Publication Data

Lindbergh, Reeve.
There's a cow in the road! / Reeve Lindbergh
pictures by Tracey Campbell Pearson. — 1st. ed.
p. cm.
Summary / A girl preparing for school is surprised by
the number of barnyard animals gathering in the road outside.
ISBN 0-8037-1335-5.—ISBN 0-8037-1336-3 (lib. bdg.)
[1. Domestic animals — Fiction.   2. Stories in rhyme.]
I. Pearson, Tracey Campbell, ill. II. Title.
PZ8.3.L6148Th 1993   [E]—dc20   91-34883   CIP   AC

The artwork was rendered in pen-and-ink and watercolor.
It was then color-separated and reproduced in full color.

Weekly Reader Children's Book Club Presents

There's a COW in the Road!

REEVE LINDBERGH

Pictures by
TRACEY CAMPBELL PEARSON

Dial Books for Young Readers NEW YORK

There's a COW in the Road!

Printed